The Goose Girl

Written by the Brothers Grimm

Retold by Livi Michael

Illustrated by Ellie Jenkins

Collins

There once was a princess who needed to marry a prince from a distant land. This was because there weren't any princes who lived nearby. So a prince was found who ruled over the land of Faraway, at the top of the Never-ending Hill.

"But it's such a long journey," said the princess. "And I don't even want to get married!"

Her mother told her she would have to get married, or she could never be a queen. And the land of Faraway was very beautiful. However, she would have to be careful not to fall down the wrong side of the Never-ending Hill, for if she did, no one would ever see her again.

The princess started to cry. "That doesn't sound nice at all," she wept. "Anyway – how will I find my way there?"

Her mother tried to cheer her up by showing her all the gold and silver that she would take with her, but the princess wouldn't stop crying until the queen said, "I'll give you a magical horse. He'll talk to you and guide you on your way."

The princess's tears dried at once, for gifts of gold and silver were one thing, and princes of distant lands another, but now she would have her very own talking horse. And a maid, who would travel with her, on her own horse.

When the day came for her to leave the princess was too excited to be sad. Her mother drew her wand over the river and a beautiful horse stepped from the sparkling water.

"His name is Falada," the queen said. "You must follow his advice. He'll be your best and wisest friend."

The horse shook his mane and said,
"Now that I am flesh and bone,
You will never be alone."

The princess clapped her hands in delight. Then she sprang up onto Falada's back. She rode around in a circle waving, and everyone was happy that she was setting off so joyfully.

Everyone, that is, apart from her maid.

"What a fuss!" she thought, watching the queen blow kisses to her daughter. "She's such a spoilt little goose!"

The maid was jealous because no one had made a fuss about her leaving, or given her any presents. And her horse was just an ordinary old nag.

But she got on it anyway and followed the princess upstream, which was the way Falada had told them to go.

They hadn't gone far before the princess began to feel thirsty. So she asked the maid, "Won't you fetch me some water in one of the golden goblets we've brought?"

"Get it yourself," said the maid.

The princess was so shocked that she meekly got off her horse and fetched her own water from the river. No one had ever spoken to her like that before. "Falada, Falada, what shall I do?" she whispered. And her horse replied,

"Drink now then ride,
Soon you'll be a bride."

Comforted by this, she climbed back onto him and stroked his mane.

But later she forgot how rude her maid had been, and asked her again for water. Once more the maid refused and said, "Get it yourself! You've got legs, haven't you?"

The princess realised that her maid wasn't going to be helpful at all. So she got down from her horse, took off her crown and cloak and her silver shoes and paddled into the river.

Cupping her hands to drink she murmured, "Falada, Falada, what shall I do?"

But the horse said nothing. And when the princess looked up, she was horrified to see her maid was sitting on him. She was even wearing the princess's cloak and crown and silver shoes!

"What's going on?" she cried. "Why are you sitting on my horse?"

"He's my horse now," said the maid.

"But my mother gave him to me!" said the princess. "And that's my cloak, and my crown and those are my silver shoes! Tell her, Falada!"

But the horse only looked sad and said, "Alas, princess, I cannot take sides. The one who rules is the one who rides."

The maid laughed, then tugged Falada's reins roughly and rode off.

The poor princess had no choice but to put on the maid's old boots and coat and cap, and climb onto the back of her ordinary old horse.

Because Falada was so fast, the maid reached the kingdom of Faraway first. She rode easily up the Never-ending Hill and everyone came out to meet her. People cheered and shouted, "Hooray for the princess!"

Falada started to protest, but the maid leaned over and whispered into his ear, "You'd better keep quiet, or I'll put a bag over your head!"

She knew that Falada would not be able to talk with a bag over his head.

Falada was very cross. He said,
"A maid you'll be and a maid you'll stay,
No matter how you make me pay!"

"We'll see about that!" said
the false princess.

Before long she came to the King
of Faraway who sat next to
his handsome son, the prince.

"My dear, we're delighted you're here," said the king. "I hope you've had a pleasant journey?"

"It was OK," said the maid, "but my horse is tired. You'll need to put him in a stable with a bag over his head – that's the only way he can get to sleep."

The king and prince were surprised by this, but they promised to do as she asked.

"Oh – and my maid'll be along in a while," added the false princess. "When she gets here make sure you give her plenty of work to do."

"What kind of work?" asked the king.

"Oh, you know – anything dirty and tiring."

"I know," said the prince, "she can help to look after the royal geese!"

And so as soon as the real princess had struggled up the Never-ending Hill on her old nag, people spoke to her as if she was her own maid! And no matter how hard she cried and claimed to be the real princess, no one believed her. She was taken to the palace yard, where she was told that she would be the grubby little Goose Boy's assistant!

Every day she had to feed the geese. Then she had to help the Goose Boy lead the geese through the higgledy-piggledy streets of the town to a meadow where they could peck about and roam freely.
They had to make sure that the geese didn't stray to the wrong side of the Never-ending Hill, where the land just fell away into nothing.

Then every day at dusk they led them back to the palace yard again.

The people of the town complained because the geese left their droppings wherever they went. The streets and alleys of Faraway were all coated with a greenish slime. The real princess apologised of course, but she didn't see how she could stop the geese from making a mess.

"They should scoop up the droppings and put them on their gardens," the Goose Boy said. "That'd make their flowers and vegetables grow."

There wasn't much that the Goose Boy didn't know about goose droppings. He talked about them a lot. The real princess tried not to mind too much. She felt sorry for him because he'd never known any other kind of life, whereas at least she'd once been a princess.

But one thing he did made her angry.

When she sat by the stream in the meadow, the real princess would often take off her maid's cap and let down her hair. Then the Goose Boy would reach out his grubby hand and try to pull out one or two of the shining strands.

The real princess would whisk her hair back under her cap. "What are you doing?" she'd cry. And the Goose Boy would hang his head and shuffle off. But the next time she shook out her shining hair, he was there again, trying to tweak some of it out.

One day the real princess got so annoyed that she stamped her foot and shouted, "Blow breezes, blow Make his hat go!"

With that a strong wind came and blew off the Goose Boy's hat! He had to chase it all the way back through the higgledy-piggledy streets, until he finally arrived at the palace.

Where he was arrested for leaving the geese.

The Goose Boy was hot and angry. He told the king about the trick the real princess had played on him.

The king was impressed that a Goose Girl could make the wind blow. As soon as she brought the geese back, he sent for her. He asked her so many questions that the whole story about the false princess came out.

Then the king sat for a while, deep in thought.

Finally he gave orders for a feast to be prepared, and for the Goose Girl to be dressed as royally as any princess.

The king sat at one end of a great table with his son and the false princess. The real princess sat at the other end. No one asked who the real princess was? The royal guests were too busy eating.

When everyone had finished eating, the old king told them the tale of the false princess, just as if it was a story he'd once heard. Then he asked the false princess what she thought should be done with such a wicked maid.

The false princess stood up.

"I think," she said, "that such a person should be put in a barrel, and rolled down the wrong side of the Never-ending Hill, and never seen again!"

Everyone looked at her in horror.

"You really are a horrid girl, aren't you?" said the king. He turned to the real princess. "What do you think?" he asked.

The real princess stood up. "I think," she said, "that such a person should be made to work as a Goose Girl and clean up all the goose droppings from the streets!"

"So be it," said the king. The king turned to the false princess. "Go and change your clothes, my dear. You wouldn't want to get goose droppings down that pretty dress."

"What? No way!" cried the false princess. "I'm not clearing up goose droppings! That's her job!"

She was still shouting as she was bundled out of the room.

The king introduced the real princess to his son. Luckily, the prince was so tired of being bossed about by the false princess that he was quite happy to meet his real bride.

The first thing the real princess did was to ask for Falada. He was led out of the stables and the bag was taken from his head. As he stood blinking in the sunlight, the real princess ran to him and put her arms around his neck. "Dear Falada!" she cried." Now you can help me to rule wisely and well!"

As for the maid, after a short time of shovelling the droppings, she went to the princess and begged her forgiveness.

"I'm sorry I was so mean," she cried. "But people will take advantage if you don't stand up for yourself!"

The princess didn't think this was much of an apology. And she wasn't prepared to let the maid avoid her punishment so easily.

"You must take all the goose droppings you've cleared from the streets and spread them on the gardens of Faraway," she said. "Then you can live in peace with your geese."

The maid told the Goose Boy he had to help her, of course. Soon the gardens of Faraway bloomed more beautifully than any gardens in the world. Then the Goose Girl and the Goose Boy settled down together to grow their own flowers and vegetables and look after their geese.

And so it can truly be said that everyone in Faraway lived happily ever after, thanks to the power of the goose droppings and the wisdom of a talking horse.

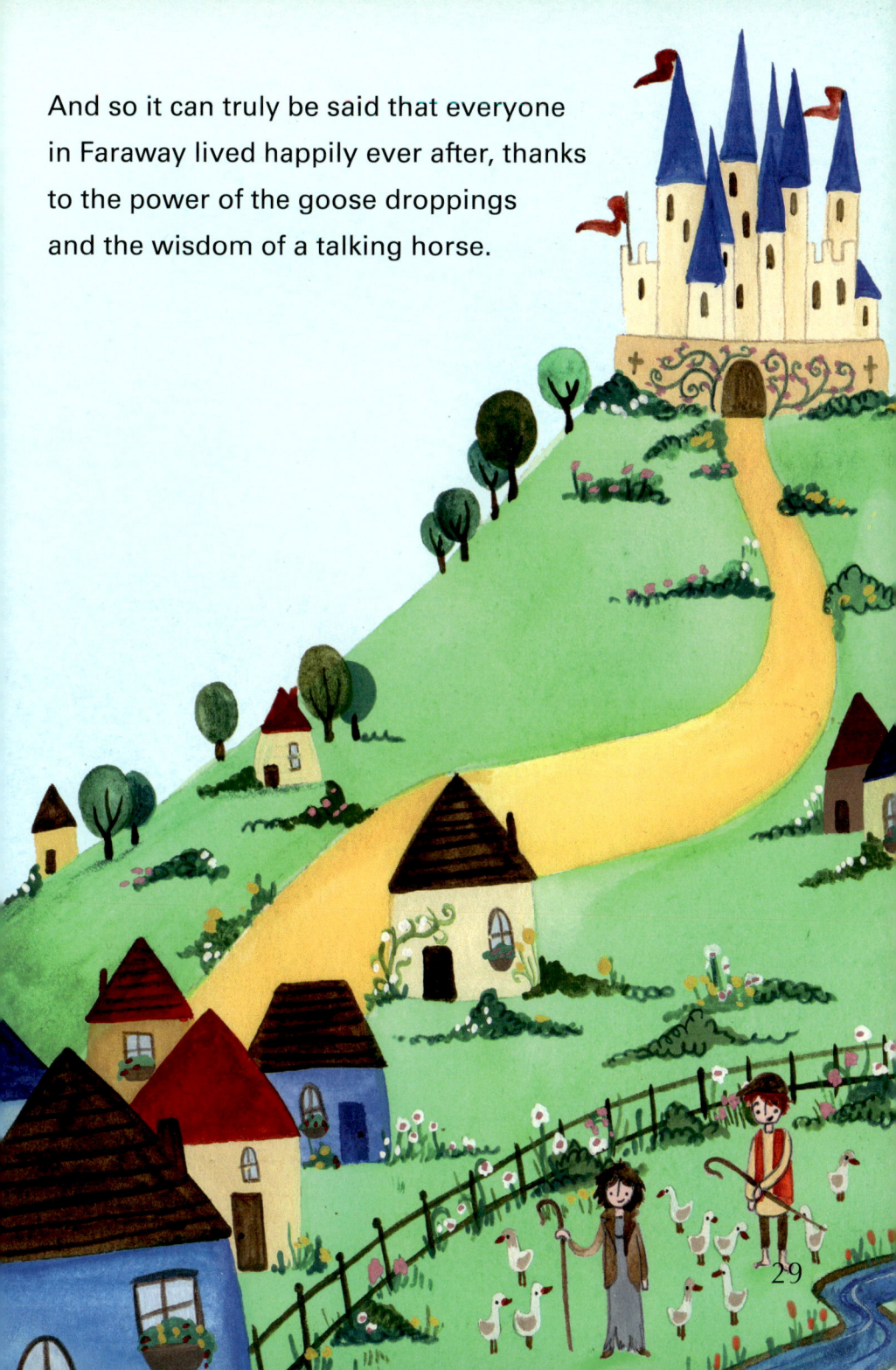

The Goose Girl's journey

The princess's kingdom

Ideas for reading

Written by Clare Dowdall, PhD
Lecturer and Primary Literacy Consultant

Reading objectives:
- increase familiarity with a wide range of books including fairy stories and retell orally
- identify themes and conventions
- discuss words and phrases that capture the reader's interest and imagination
- make predictions from details stated and applied

Spoken language objectives:
- use spoken language to develop understanding through speculating, hypothesising, imagining and exploring ideas

Curriculum Links: PSHE

Resources: paper and pens for drawing and writing; voice recorder

Build a context for reading
- Look at the front cover together. Read the title and discuss the illustration. Ask the children why they think that the girl has a sad expression on her face.
- Read the blurb. Challenge children to make connections between the information provided and the girl on the front cover. Help them to imagine what's happened to the Princess and her horse.
- Explain that this is a famous fairy story based on the tale by the Brothers Grimm.

Understand and apply reading strategies
- Read pp2–5 with the children. Ask them what kind of story this will be and what conventions it will contain (e.g. magical creatures and events, a happy ending, a wicked character, princes and princesses).
- Ask children to look closely at the language used and to identify words and phrases that are used in fairy and folk tales.